J. Beard

Little Workers

Anatiposi

J. Beard

Little Workers

Reprint of the original.

1st Edition 2023 | ISBN: 978-3-38211-102-1

Anatiposi Verlag is an imprint of Outlook Verlagsgesellschaft mbH.

Verlag (Publisher): Outlook Verlag GmbH, Zeilweg 44, 60439 Frankfurt, Deutschland
Vertretungsberechtigt (Authorized to represent): E. Roepke, Zeilweg 44, 60439 Frankfurt, Deutschland
Druck (Print): Books on Demand GmbH, In de Tarpen 42, 22848 Norderstedt, Deutschland

LITTLE WORKERS.

A HISTORY OF SOME OF

God's Little Creatures

THAT

LABOR WITHOUT HANDS.

BY J. C. BEARD.

R. SHUGG & CO., Publishers,
53 Chatham St., New York.

1871.

LITTLE
WORKERS

Published by R. Shugg & Co.

NEW YORK

TABLE OF CONTENTS.

INTRODUCTION.

How often have children been heard to wish that the stories they read of Fairies were true, and that they could find among the flowers little fairy people, dancing in the moonlight, or doing their fairy work with tiny tools in the small houses they have built, of leaves and moss, half hidden among buds and blossoms? Now, for all such we have very good news. In this strange world of ours, where grown up people as well as children are always finding something new, some learned men have discovered that, although no fairies just such as the story-books tell about are to be found, there are whole nations of little beings gifted with life, activity and intelligence, who live their little lives very much after the fashion of the Fairies. Among these little people are found, as among us larger folks, carpenters, plasterers, masons, soldiers, musicians, confectioners, silk-weavers, paper-makers, boat-builders, cattle-raisers, butchers, magicians, torch-bearers, tent-makers, tailors, divers, architects, with many others, in fact nearly all the trades known to us, and some that are not.

In this work, under the guise of fiction, we have endeavored to remove the erroneous and disagreeable impressions that are often forced upon children respecting a large portion of our Heavenly Father's exquisite creations. To teach facts in science is not our aim, except so far as shall awaken interest in the opening minds of our children, and excite their curiosity to know more of the most fascinating branches of human knowledge. It is our belief, however, that there is little in the general results of scientific research that cannot be made perfectly clear to the understanding of even young children, if the right method be rightly employed. It is often said, and well said, that "fact is stranger than fiction," and it may well be added that the more interesting its presentation the more readily it is comprehended. If we first parade a catalogue of incomprehensible names, technical words, and formal statements, the intellect is bewildered and repelled; but in the very fact that the truths of the material creation do not necessarily consist in or rest upon a scientific nomenclature, however useful, lies the possibility of so presenting knowledge that a child may mentally assimilate it, and acquire an appetite for future researches.

We are apt to think that we have done wonderful things, and point to the Pyramids, the temples, the roads, the walls, the mines and the tunnels we have built as evidences of our skill and industry; but the insects, taking their size into account, have far out-stripped us. We shall have to dig a tunnel under the Atlantic Ocean, and connect America with Europe by a road under the water, sink shafts thirty miles straight down into the earth, and erect buildings as large as mountains, if we attempt to equal their ordinary works. We could tell you more about them, how they lay concrete pavements in their cities, how they sow grain and gather it, how industrious and helpful they are, each one and each class having its own appointed place and labor; but I hope I have raised enough curiosity on your part, my dear little readers, to set you at work to look for these little folks in the gardens and fields to which you have access. There, if you watch them closely, you will see that all I have told you is true, and will learn that no work of God is insignificant or unworthy of your notice.

BUTTERFLIES.

GEORGE was a bright little fellow about ten years old when his parents moved from the great city in which they had lived ever since George could remember, into a house his father had bought in a beautiful place called Rutherford Park, a little distance from New York City. As you may imagine, this was a great event in Master George's life. To eat strawberries, raspberries, and black-berries from the very vines upon which they grew; to find little birds'-nests containing real eggs, or better still a brood of nestlings; to wander under the grand old trees where no signs were put up to forbid him walking on the grass or wandering knee-deep in the clover;—these seemed to George the greatest of pleasures. But he liked best of all the bright-winged Butterflies, for he had a confused belief that they were flowers endowed with animal life and motion. He also noticed the Caterpillars on the leaves and blossoms, but he did not know at first that they had anything to do with But-terflies.

A short time after their arrival at their new home, George's father took him to see an old gentle-man, who among other things showed them a Vivarium. This the gentleman said was intended for the rearing of insects of the water as well as land. A portion of the interior was set apart as a reservoir, the water curving back from the front of the case in the form of a little bay. The water-tight separation forming this little bay consisted of a flat piece of metal fastened to the bottom of the Vivarium. The old gentleman gave them quite a description of how it was made; he told them that the reservoir at its bottom and sides was formed of zinc and its front of glass. The water occu-pied half of the depth of the Vivarium, leaving plenty of room for the land part. At the sides and back the zinc came up to the water level, and above this the whole top lifted off, so as to allow of cleaning and ventilating at such times as the insects were not in a flying state. The upper portion fitted tightly, sinking into a deep groove cut all around the top edge of the lower portion. The sides of the upper portion were pierced with little holes to admit air, and these sides also formed the frame-work of a glass door, admitting access to all portions; this door occupied all the remaining part of the Vivarium above the little bay. The back was the same except that there was no door. Above all this again came the roof, which was also of zinc pierced with little holes. This roof was shaped something like what house-builders call the Mansard, and quite fancifully ornamented. The land part of the Vivarium inclined upward from the water, and had the appearance of a little hill. At the bottom of the little bay the old gentleman had put little piles of stones and tiny flower-pots in which were growing water plants, the whole bed or bottom of the bay being covered with little pebbles and fine white sand. As soon as the plants get large, the old gentleman said, he removes them, for if left to grow they would soon fill up the tank. He had also some pond snails in the water, as he explained, to act as scavengers, for they eat up all the decaying plants and thereby help to keep the water clean and sweet. In making the land the old gentleman said he had first put in little pieces of brick and broken flower-pots to the depth of about three inches, so that part of the earth was dry, for some of the insects do not thrive where it is damp; then he sowed common grass seed on the earth placed over the broken brick, with little tufty plants and some ferns. But first into the earth were placed little bottles filled with water, into which he put the stalks of certain plants upon which the Caterpillar feeds, the water in the bottles serving to keep the stalks fresh and green. Beside these little bottles there were planted some pots containing bright flowering plants, which served as food for the Butterflies, and also gave the Vivarium a pleasant and beautiful appearance.

This Vivarium George was delighted with. "I have seen little birds in cages and fishes in globes," said George, "but I never before saw a Butterfly's house."

"Please, sir," said he, "perhaps you can tell me where the Butterflies come from. I have found young birds and the shells they had come out of in the nests built by the old ones; but I have never found any little, tiny, young Butterflies. They all seem to be grown up."

The old gentleman smiled and patted George on the head. "Do you see those creatures on the thistle leaves?" said he.

"Oh!" replied George, "the Caterpillars?"

"Yes," said the old gentleman, "they are the larvæ of the Butterfly."

George did not understand this very well, but he did not like to say so.

"Do you see the chrysalis on the plants?" said the old gentleman, directing George's attention to some small objects that looked like bundles of seed hanging here and there among the plants.

"Yes, sir," said George.

"Then," said the gentleman, "you see the long and short of the transformation of the pupa of Lepidopteros insects into the winged Imago."

"Yes, sir," said George, looking blank, "but where is it?"

"What?" asked the gentleman.

"Why that thing, that winged Imago, and the chrysalis, and the Pupa?"

"I am afraid my little son does not quite understand you," said George's father, smiling.

"To be sure he does not," said the gentleman; "I was trying the book method on the little fellow. Some folks think that nothing can be learned about nature without first knowing all the hard names that men of science have fastened upon her. Now we will try another way."

The old gentleman took George upon his knee, and patting his head kindly, said, "Do you know what happens to a seed when it is put into the ground?"

"What kind of a seed?" said George.

"Almost any kind," said his friend, "a kernel of corn, for instance."

"The chickens get it sometimes—they ate up all the pop-corn I planted," said master George.

"But if the chickens do not get it?" said the old gentleman, humoring his little friend.

"Why, then" said George slowly, as though he did not like to give it up, "they begin to sprout."

"Exactly!" said his friend; "and a great plant or tree grows from the little seed, and bears beautiful flowers or delicious fruit. What happens to us when we die, as we all must do at some time, and are put into the ground?"

"We turn into angels," said the little fellow.

"All of us?" asked the old gentleman gravely.

"No;" replied George, "only good people."

"How do you know that what you have told me is true?" asked George's questioner.

"My father told me so;—and it is printed in the bible," added George, after a moment's thought.

"Well," said the old gentleman, "you have answered my questions so readily and correctly that I will answer yours, and tell you where the Butterflies come from. Now the Caterpillars, the ugly, crawling Caterpillars you see there, George, all become Butterflies. At first they are nothing but a seed or an egg, for an egg is the same to an insect that the seed is to a plant; from the one grows a tree, perhaps, and from the other issues an insect or bird; the trees grow up, bursting into bloom, and become great boquets of gaily colored flowers and perfume; the egg, at the time set for it, changes into a beautiful winged creature. The eggs that hatch into Caterpillars, however, are not like birds' eggs, they are far more beautiful." Here the old gentleman showed George the drawings of a few of them very much enlarged or magnified from the real ones; some were as round as a ball, others were oval shaped, others again shaped like bits of pipe-stem, and still others like sugar loaves. George said he would never have thought them to be eggs from their appearance, and I do not think our little readers would either from the picture on the next page. You will notice how beautifully figured and carved they are, while birds' eggs are perfectly smooth. Indeed it will always be found in the works of the great Creator, that the smaller they are the more beautiful and finished they appear to be, which is just the opposite in regard to the works of men.

BUTTERFLIES' EGGS.

" When the Caterpillar is born," resumed the old gentleman, " his business, like that of the human baby, is to eat and sleep. Watch that greedy fellow there on the thistle; see how busy he is. He will perhaps eat double his weight of food in a day and night; think, George, of a well-grown little fellow like you eating one hundred and twenty pounds of beefsteak, bread and vegetables in twenty-four hours. Indeed, if our children had appetites in proportion to those of Caterpillars, they would soon eat us out of house and home, and cause a universal famine. Providentially, however, the larger animals are smaller eaters. But small as the race of insects are, they sometimes do infinite harm to vegetation, and if there were not so many killed by birds and animals and by rains and storms, they would eat up every green thing upon the face of the whole earth. Do you notice, George, the Caterpillars you see, though different in shape and size, are in some respects alike? They are all long and round, and are divided by deep creases, as if they had been tied tightly around a dozen separate parts of their bodies. You notice, too, how soft they are, so that they can draw out, or shorten, or put themselves in any required position, along crooked branches or leaves, to get their food. What strange looking creatures they would be if they were as large as the cows and horses that pasture in the fields. They would be frightful beings, with their great blind-looking faces, and from four to six small, strangely formed eyes in circles on the back of the head, terrible jaws armed with teeth that instead of working up and down as ours do, open and shut sideways. Yet they are a great deal like human beings in some things. I don't mean with respect to their outward shape, but to the changes they undergo. Our Heavenly Father made them, and meant them as a sign and a figure of the changes that take place in all human beings. You told me just now, George, that people when they were put into the ground, if they lived as God meant they should live, turned into angels, and you said that the bible told you so. Now, George, not only God's written but his *created* word will tell you so too, for the Creator has written his bible not alone in a book but in flowers, and leaves, and insects, and stars, and in everything he has made; and if we know how to read his great book of nature, we will understand his little bible a great deal better, and if we love his written word, we will love every work of his hand, and will try to understand what he meant to teach us in each one. Now these little.

worms as well as ourselves, for we too are but worms before God, suffer a change, and from the eager, greedy, crawling creature you see destroying the beautiful plants, becomes, by what to it is a sort of death, a glorified creature, that is no more like the thing it once was than a flower is like a seed Instead of lurking in obscure corners and groveling near the earth, it lives and moves only in the pure air and bright sunshine, when the flowers are in their fullest bloom and the earth is most like the paradise it once was, before sin brought blight and ruin upon it."

Little George listened with flushed cheeks and wondering eyes. His beloved Butterflies were indeed well worth loving if all that the kind old gentleman had told him about them were true. He looked silently for a while upon them as they moved contentedly about in their beautiful home, and then said in a low voice: "Then the Butterflies are Caterpillar's angels?"

George's friend smiled, but did not contradict him.

"But," said George, "they die when the cold weather comes."

The old gentleman stopped smiling and turned to George's father: "This shows how we are carried away by fancy into error. I was wrong, my little friend," he continued, speaking to George, "to let you call them angels. The angels of the human race are true, real, living beings, who never die; but these little creatures are only the sign and show of something, as written words or pictures are the sign and show of the ideas they represent."

"See what is written here," said the old gentleman, showing George a little card.

"It is a verse out of the testament," said George promptly, for he was a good scholar for his age, and was a little vain of his proficiency.

"*That which is born of the flesh is flesh; and that which is born of the spirit is spirit.*"

"See," said the old gentleman; "I am going to destroy that verse of testament;" and he tore the card to bits. "Now," said he, "there is no longer such a verse."

"Indeed," said George, "you only tore the card; but I can read the same verse out of my little testament at home. Nobody can destroy God's word."

"Truth itself!" said the old gentleman. "The wisest man who lives could not have answered better. Well, it is the same with the Butterflies; they are only a beautiful living sign and show of something that is far more real and beautiful. The sign and show can be destroyed, but its meaning exists forever."

"Were all the Butterflies once Caterpillars?" asked George.

"Yes," replied his friend, "every one;—that is to say, every Butterfly was once in a Caterpillar form; for as our soul exists in us from the moment we are born, so the perfect Butterfly lives in the Caterpillar. The Caterpillar is in fact a Butterfly wrapped up and packed away in a worm. When it bursts forth perfect in all its parts the outside worm-body is thrown away, and what it contained comes forth perfected and glorified. But first the Caterpillar has to suffer its sort of death; it ceases to eat, and seeks some sheltered place, and, in the case of some moths, spins itself a sort of winding sheet or cocoon, or attaches itself by a web and hangs suspended, as you see on the branches of the plants in the Vivarium, a lifeless-looking, motionless bundle, without legs, wings or eyes. As the time draws near for the insect to escape from its earthy prison, its outside covering or external part becomes somewhat transparent, and the form and even the markings of the future Butterfly can be more or less plainly seen. But you cannot judge from the Caterpillar what kind of Butterfly is contained in it, for some plain, sober worms become brilliant Butterflies, while showy, bright-colored Caterpillars will often turn out to be common-looking moths. Like men, their inner selves are not to be judged from their outward looks. It is impossible to determine until the perfect insect appears what it will be like Sometimes the Caterpillars are stung by small flies that lay eggs underneath the Caterpillar's skin, which eggs hatch into worms that eat away all the fat of the Caterpillar, and thus destroys the Butterfly before it has reached perfection. The worms also spin little cocoons all over the Caterpillar's back, as you see in the picture; this makes him look very fine, but it is a sign that he is never to mount up on silver wings into the pleasant air and sunshine. Some Caterpillars go through life safely, and enter the chrysalis state in full health; but when the time comes for the Butterfly to appear, there comes forth instead a terrible looking creature whose sole business in life is to prey upon other Caterpillars."

George was so much interested in what he had heard of the Butterflies, that the gentleman afterwards told him a great deal more about the lives of other little beings that we call insects; but as George had already made quite a lengthy stay, his father decided that it was time to go home, and although he had been so interested in what the old gentleman had told him, he bid his new-found friend a cheerful good-bye, after receiving a cordial invitation to come again, when he was promised a further narration of the habits and lives of some of the little creatures that form part of the insect world, and are God's *Little Workers*, sent to show us his wondrous wisdom and greatness even in little things.

MOTHS.

George had been so much interested in the old gentleman's account of his Butterflies that he longed to hear more, and when he next visited his friend asked him to tell him something else about the Butterflies.

"I could indeed tell you a great deal more about them," said the old gentleman, "but perhaps I had better now give you some account of a different kind of insect that is very much like the Butterfly; so much so, in fact, that it is sometimes hard to tell one from the other;—I mean Moths. I have just received a fine collection of these interesting insects, which I will show you if you would like to see them."

George said that he would like it very much, and followed the old gentleman into his cabinet; George called it the museum. It was a large room with glass-covered stands about it, like those our little readers may have seen upon store counters, only instead of containing articles such as are there exhibited for sale, these were full of beautiful shells, insects, and minerals or stones. Around this strange-looking room were also shelves, on which were arranged more books than George had ever seen in one room before. At the sides and on the top of the cases of books, shelves were placed on which were stuffed birds with varnished legs and bright glass eyes; great white Swans were there, and black ones too for that matter; Auks and Geese from the far north; scarlet Flamingoes, having bills that no other bird could possibly know what to do with. A large case containing Ferns stood at one window; a still larger one with a tank well stocked with fish and water-plants at another, the Vivarium of insects at the third, and at the fourth and remaining one a sort of double easy-chair or settle covered with green morocco, and a table at which the old gentleman studied or wrote. Here George and his friend were accustomed to sit together; and now the old gentleman taking a large case from a drawer placed it on the table. If it had been made of gold he could not have handled it more carefully or seemed more proud of it; and yet it only contained a lot of Moths with pins stuck through their backs;—dried insects, "of no earthly use or benefit to anybody," some persons might think. George did not say so because, perhaps, he was impressed by the old gentleman's manner of treating his treasure; for if ever we expect others to value our productions, possessions, or character, we must appear to value them ourselves.

"Oh, how beautiful!" exclaimed George; and indeed if a gallery of pictures by the best of the old masters, works of art that could not be bought, no, not if you should cover the canvass with gold pieces, invokes from the beholder such an exclamation, surely these paintings of the oldest and greatest of all masters might well do so. Such a perfect blending of strength and softness in the colors; such an artful and artistic keeping down in sober gray or dull black of a whole wing in order to bring into vivid relief a spot or marking where the very purest and brightest tints on the pallette of nature was lavished; such exquisite finish in the pencelling and mottling and clouding of some, and such a rich contrast of complimentary colors—orange and blue, yellow and purple, red and green—on others, surely challenges every human effort at competition or imitation.

"What a pity it is that the color comes off their wings so easily," said George. "It is just dusted on, and sticks to my fingers when I touch them."

"That which appears to you to be dust, George," said his friend, "is really the feathers, or rather I should say the scales of the Butterfly. See, I have my pocket microscope on the table, and will put in a slide containing some of the wing dust. Now look!"

"Oh!" said George; "I see a whole lot of little things like differently shaped fans!"

"Those are the scales or feathers I told you of; they are so small that to the naked eye they look like dust," said the old gentleman.

"They don't look much like scales; and they don't look at all like feathers," said George.

"But they are scales," replied his friend. "Scales, you know, may have different shapes. At any rate they answer the same purpose to the Butterfly and Moth that hair does to the quadruped,

feathers to birds and scales to fish. They are fastened to the wings by the little stems you see growing out of them, and usually overlap each other like the shingles on a house-roof. There are, it is said, about one hundred thousand seven hundred and thirty-six to every square inch of Moth or Butterfly; and every one of these little bits of tiny littleness is infinitely more carefully made than the finest lady's fan you or anybody else has ever seen." The old gentle-

MOTHS' SCALES.

man was justly proud of his case of Moths, for some of them had been sent to him from countries far over the ocean—from India, from South America, from Australia and from Europe. There was a rare and highly valued specimen of the magnificent African Moth with its beautiful crimson wings bordered with broad black and white spotted bands—the *Callimorpha Helcita*, shown at No. 1 on our colored plate. Near it was the splendidly colored Great American Moth of Georgia,—*Doricampa Regalis*, No. 2,—with its out-spread wings all ablaze with scarlet, yellow, and glossy black, yielding place for size and beauty to no Moth on the face of the earth.

Above these George saw the little British Plumed Moths,—Nos. 3 and 4,—whose wings are made up of separate feathers like those of a bird ; and below on the right,—No. 5,—another foreigner, and a very questionable looking one at that, with dark funereal wings and fierce aspect.

" Why," said George, " it has a skeleton on its back ; skull and backbone, ribs and all ! "

" So it has," said the old gentleman, " and it is therefore called the Death's Head Moth."

" Do you think it just happened so ? " said George, " or that it was really meant for a skeleton ? "

" I do not think anything 'just happened so,'" replied his friend. " The slightest and most obscure markings on a Moth or Butterfly have their purpose and meaning, and the Creator uses their wings as little pages upon which he writes or paints so many beautiful lessons that no man can ever in this world learn all they teach, though he study them his lifetime. You can see for yourself in this case that the skull is not only marked out and finished, but there is an indication of the collar bone and ribs. The people of Poland, where this one came from, call them ' Death's Head Phantoms,' ' Wandering Death-Birds,' and other horrible names. Of course they are really quite harmless, though they have often frightened the ignorant and superstitious country people in those places in Europe where they abound. They utter a dismal squeak when they are taken, although how they do it puzzles the scientific men ; for you must know that insects breathe through holes in their sides instead of through their mouths or nostrils as we do, and so they can scarcely have such a thing as a voice."

" I know that fellow," said George, pointing to one we have figured as No. 6 ; " he comes buzzing around the flowers in the evening. We call him a Hum-bug, because he makes a sort of a humming noise, and pretends he is a Humming-bird."

The old gentleman smiled at George's description. " Yes," said he, " that is called the Humming-bird Moth. We have Humming-bird Moths ; but this little fellow is an Englishman. You see his wings are translucent like those of a fly. He hides himself among the leaves during the heat of the day, but as soon as the shades of evening appear, he darts about from flower to flower and poises like a Humming-bird over the blossoms until he has sucked out all the honey with his long curled trunk or proboscis."

" But," said George, " what are those ugly, clumsy fellows with such ill-shaped wings and fat bodies ? I cannot see what right they have among so many beautiful creatures."

" And yet, George," replied his friend, " like many homely people and things, these misshapen, clumsy looking insects serve mankind more usefully and are of far more value to us than all the bright colored insects the tropics can produce. It is true they themselves are far from beautiful ; but it is from the material they weave that the ladies dress themselves in such bright and shining garments, and deck themselves with ribbons and keep out the cold of winter with rich, soft velvets; for these, George, are the Moths of the celebrated Silk-worm,—*Bombye Mori*, as the book-makers call them." These our little readers will see figured at Nos. 7 and 8 on the accompanying plate.

"Near them," continued George's friend, "you will see their cocoons, (Nos. 9 and 10,) from one of which the Moth is crawling. It is from these all the silk is unwound. When one of the Silk-worm Caterpillars has lived thirty-two days, and cast off its skin four times, it begins to spin its shroud of silk. In doing this it takes a great deal of care, and observes a regular order that is always the same, and which ends in its being wrapped up in a ball of fine silken thread, which, when stretched out, is almost half a mile in length. And yet it takes more than ten thousand cocoons to make five pounds of silk, as a single cocoon with its two thousand feet of thread will weigh but three grains and a half. When we think of the great quantity of silk that is used at the present day, the number of these little worms engaged in the manufacture of the raw material is almost beyond computation. The Silk-worms came at first from the same place from which so many wonderful things came to us originally,—the mariner's compass, printing, gunpowder, porcelain and tea among other things. Of course you know I mean China. The invention of silk, or how to manufacture it from the web of a Caterpillar, was made by a lady, which fact goes to prove that ladies can be inventors and discovers after all. This lady was a Chinese Empress named Su-ling-shi, and her husband, the Emperor's, name was Ho-ang-ti, which rhymes very well with hers; he, however, is only remembered from the fact that he was Su-ling-shi's husband. This ingenious Empress not only taught the ladies of her court how to raise and take care of the Silk-worms, but also how to weave the fabric afterwards; and so she set the fashion, and everybody followed it, and silk became so common that the laboring people wore it. This is all supposed to have happened about three thousand years ago, and the Silk-worms have gone on making silk ever since. Silk soon found its way into Europe, but for a long time no one knew how it was made nor what it was made of, until at last, about one thousand three hundred years ago, a couple of monks who happened to be in India, where, as well as in China silk has been produced for no one knows how long, found out how it was made, and wished to take some of the silk-producing worms back to Europe with them; but the natives, who were afraid that if the secret of making silk became known and the means of manufacturing it were afforded they would no longer get such high prices for it, refused to let any of the Caterpillars be taken away. However the sly monks were not to be baulked in that way, and hid some of the insects in hollow canes, and marching off unsuspected, introduced the culture of silk into Greece so successfully that some four hundred years afterwards the Europeans had all they wanted from Constantinople, and bought no more in India. You will see from this circumstance how God watches over the interests of his children, and how he will not allow his gifts to man, which he means for the benefit of the whole human race, to be used for the profit of a comparatively small number."

George was as much interested in his friend's account of the Moths as he had been in that of the Butterflies, and thanked him very much for his kindness. He showed such an evident desire to learn, that the old gentleman took pleasure in imparting what he knew, and invited George to accompany him upon an excursion which he contemplated soon making, when he promised to give him an insight into the life and habits of another insect, an account of which will be given in the next chapter

SPIDERS.

One bright, sunshiny day George accompanied his old friend the Entomologist on a hunting excursion. They carried neither gun nor amunition, nor had they a hunting dog at their heels; the only implements of destruction they had were one small vial of chloroform, two jars of alcohol, half a dozen pill-boxes, and a snare made of mosquito netting sewed to a hoop at the end of a long pole. These, however, were amply sufficient for the capture of the game they sought, which was Spiders. Many persons, perhaps, would think that hunting Spiders was neither a very sensible or profitable occupation; but George and his friend had a different opinion, and had good reason to expect to be both richer and wiser from their excursion. George, at least, fulfilled the first expectation; and so indeed, I am safe to say, did the old gentleman; for no one, not even the wisest, can study either God's created or written word in the right spirit, without carrying away from it some new truth. Besides, the old gentleman succeeded in securing specimens for a book he was preparing on American Spiders, among which specimens were one or two he could not have bought for any amount of money, because they had never been noticed before; so he was richer as well as wiser. During the journey, which was like a walk through a great museum of wonders to George, so interesting had each insect, leaf and flower become, as his friend told him how they grew and lived, and described many beautiful and curious things that he would never have guessed concerning them. But the old gentleman spoke principally of the Spiders, and was never tired of telling George about their industry and ingenuity,—how they spread their snares, protect their young, and in some instances take care of them until they are able to gain a living for themselves. "They are different from other insects," said he, "for, as I have already told you, nearly all insects breathe through holes in their sides, while the breathing-place of the Spider is underneath the body. Besides, Spiders have hearts, which other insects do not have."

"I don't see how anything can live without a heart," said George.

"No warm-blooded animal can live without a heart, in strict truth; though some people, who seem to have no more human feeling than these insects, are said to be cold-blooded and heartless," replied his friend.

"Isn't the blood in any insects warm?" asked George.

"No;" replied his friend; "no insect or reptile has warm blood. Insects have neither hearts, lungs, nor bones, though they have some things that supply the place of all these. They all undergo changes, which are called transformations, and which completely alter their form."

"I know;" said George; "the same as you told me about the Caterpillars changing into Butterflies."

"They have six legs," continued the old gentleman, "two feelers or antennæ, and two eyes, or a collection of many little eyes placed close together like the cells in a honey-comb. Now Spiders differ from other insects in all these respects; they not only have a heart and a different breathing apparatus, but they have eight legs instead of six, are without antennæ, and they are born in their final shapes, instead of changing like other insects. Another difference is that other insects after they have come into their proper form never grow, while Spiders do. You will also notice that the head and body are all one, while other insects have a division between the two. For these reasons authorities differ as to whether they should be classed as insects or animals."

They were talking about these things, when suddenly George uttered a cry, and pointed out a queer, active, little, crab-like creature, striped like a Zebra, that was on a large gray rock that towered up on one side of the road, evidently interested in the manœuvres of a large fly that was stretching out a pair of legs in front of his head and rubbing them together and then smoothing down his wings with a hinder pair, after the manner of flies when making their toilets. Master Speckleback would sidle up a little way, and then as the fly, evidently annoyed at the stranger's attention made a movement, would start off at a great rate sideways or backward, for he seemed able to run one way as well as another, and pretend to be after something else altogether and not to be thinking about the fly at all. At last master fly took a little walk, as flies do, making perhaps a dozen or so steps in one direction, stopping, and then going on again in another for a little way, trying this spot and then that, to see if he could find anything fit for a fly to eat.

"Oh, see the coward!" said George indignantly, as the little striped creature, which his friend told him was a hunting Spider, scuttled off when the fly happened to approach it.

"Wait;" said his friend; "the Spider is no coward, only he does not wish to startle his prey and make him fly off." As he spoke the fly came to a stop; he had found something, perhaps a drop of moisture too small to be seen by the human eye, and was busy sucking it up through his trunk. The Spider saw his chance; creeping up so softly and slowly that George could only see he moved by the gradually lessening distance between the two creatures, he at last with a sudden spring threw himself upon the fly, and despite his frantic struggles pinned him fast and proceeded to devour him at his leisure.

George was very much interested in watching this episode, and he asked the old gentleman why the little striped tiger prowled around like a cat after birds, instead of spinning a web and waiting for its prey to come into it?

" It seeks its prey as nature teaches it," was the reply.   " It can spin a web, however, and indeed does construct a sort of nest or chamber in which it lives.   But if this kind of Spider seems to do so little in the way of web spinning, there is another, the name of which is *Agelena Labyrinthica*, whose web is so large that it spreads out like a broad sheet, over grass, low vines and bushes.   The middle of the sheet, which is woven fine and close, is slung like a sailor's hammock, by silken ropes stretched out and fastened to the higher branches; it all slopes in one direction, ending in a long funnel-shaped gallery which is nearly level at first, but soon winds more and more steeply down until it becomes perpendicular.   The gallery is about a quarter of an inch in diameter, more closely woven than the sheet of the web, and sometimes descends into a hole in the ground, but more often into a group of crowded twigs or a tuft of grass.   Here the Spider lives in safety, with its long legs stretched out from the entrance of the gallery, ready to spring upon any insect that may happen to fall into its net."

" Are there any other kinds of Spiders beside these, that do not weave webs?" asked George.

" Oh yes;" replied his friend.   " I have some specimens at home which I will show you if you like, of Spiders that live under water in diving bells of their own construction ; as well as one that, like the boy in the nursery rhyme, 'lives by himself' in a little mud cabin, with a door in it that opens and shuts.   Here are some colored engravings of these Spiders," said the old gentleman, seating himself on a fallen tree and taking a book from his pocket.   George, who was not so unlike other children as to have any objection to looking at pictures, seated himself by the old gentleman's side.

" This individual," said his friend, indicating with his finger the Spider which our little readers will find in the lower right hand corner of the accompanying plate, No. 1, " is called the Diving Water Spider.   It builds a little dome of closely woven silk in the shape of a large thimble, or half the shell of a pigeon's egg, or like a diving-bell.   This is sometimes left partly above the water, but at others is entirely beneath the surface, and is always fastened to the objects near it by a great number of little silken cables.   It is closed all around but has an opening below.   Here Lady Spinner lays a number of eggs, which she keeps in a yellow bag and fills up a fourth part of her chamber.   But the strangest part of the story is that these Spiders are air-breathing insects, and by means of some secret of nature, which learned men have never been able to find out, they carry a supply of air down into the water with them, This air surrounds them with a bubble that shines like quicksilver. They fill their little houses with air by taking down bubble after bubble, and thus store such a supply in the hollow dome as entirely forces the water out of it."

"This other one," continued the old gentleman, turning over a page and pointing to the one that figures in the left hand corner of our plate as No. 2, "is the fellow that lives in a hut built of mud, in a style equal if not superior to some savage nations of the human race. The hut has a fine door to it that opens and shuts with spring hinges." Here the old gentleman read for George the description given in his book of this Spider.

"What bright colors some of these Spiders have; see those fellows all green and yellow and scarlet," said George, pointing to the pictures of the *Sparassus Sma-rag-du-lus*, figured as No. 8 on our plate.

"What a name!" said George, as the old gentleman told him it.

"Yes," said his friend, "and see the handsome tints and markings of these others, less brilliant but far more delicate and beautiful than the *Sparassus*."

"I thought Spiders were always dingy, dirty, long-legged things, with fat ugly bodies. I never supposed there was much that was nice or interesting about them," said George.

"That is because your eyes have not yet been trained to see the beautiful in nature," said the old gentleman. "There are very many people like you. Nature, like everything else, has to be studied to be appreciated."

"I don't think I know the meaning of such big words," said George.

"Well, I will tell you what I mean: nature is like a beautiful story book; to a savage or to an ignorant person it is only a number of pieces of paper glued or sewed together, and covered with little black marks that are not pictures of anything, and look like nothing that he ever saw elsewhere."

"You mean the letters and words," said George.

"Yes," said his friend, "to you they are words and call up beautiful pictures, or describe distant lands, or relate wonderful histories, and sometimes they make you laugh and sometimes cry, but to the savage they are without purpose or meaning. So it is with God's great book of the creation; to those who study and love it, it is more interesting than anything that can be told in words, but to careless and ignorant eyes it means little or nothing."

George understood his friend sufficiently to say that he never intended to be careless or idle, or despise the beautiful things with which the great Creator had filled the world to amuse and instruct his children. Of course in saying this he used different words, but his companion understood him very well.

" When we look at the sticky gum," said his friend, "which the Spiders draw out of their bodies to form their lines and webs, and the rough, hairy covering of most of them, we might very well conclude that they would always be dirty and full of dust and covered with flakes of whitewash or plaster, or stuck all over with bits of the webs they spin. This indeed would be the case if they were not very careful; but a Spider will seldom or never leave a thread of its web to dangle down like the untidy lacing of a sloven's shoe, but when it has no further use for a line it rolls it up into a little ball and throws it away. Its claws are just the thing for this as well as for gliding along the lines, and I tell you that Blondin, the Frenchman, who walked over Niagara Falls on a bridge made

of a single rope, was no such performer on the tight-rope as our Spider. The Spider has three claws, one of which serves as a thumb, the other two have teeth like a comb." The old gentleman showed George a picture of a Spider's claw, greatly magnified, which we here reproduce. "The long hairy legs of the Spider," continued the old gentleman, "are always catching bits of web and specks of dust; but these are cleaned carefully away, and when a Spider seems to be resting idly, in nine cases out of ten it is engaged in slowly combing its legs with its mandibles, which have teeth

SPIDER'S CLAW.   like the claws on its feet. The web which the Spider spins and which seems to be composed of a single thread, is in fact made up of many. Beneath the Spider's body is a strange

looking affair called a spinneret, consisting of five sacks covered with rows of little bristle-like points. Each one of these tiny points, (compared with which the point of the finest needle is a blunt bar of metal,) is hollow, and sends out a thread so extremely fine that it would in some cases take four millions of them to make a thread as thick as one of the hairs on your head; and all these little threads are combined to make a single line of a Spider's web. Indeed some Spiders take advantage of the wonderful fineness and brightness of their threads to fly without wings."

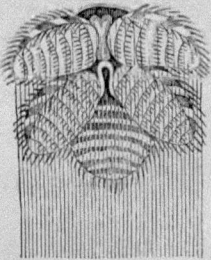

SPIDER'S SPINNERET.

" Can Spiders fly ?" asked George.   " I never knew that before."

" Indeed they can ;" answered the old gentleman ; " or perhaps I should say they float through the air, as men do in balloons."

" Well," said George, "that is stranger yet if they can make balloons."

" Yes;" said his friend ; " but you must not think that they have bags filled with gas as men have in order to ascend ; their balloons are more on the plan of those that boys make of paper by tying strings at the corners of a square sheet and then fastening a weight of some kind to the cords, and letting it out of a window for the wind to carry up. The scientific name of this kind of balloon is 'Parachute,'"

"But they are not very good balloons," said George somewhat disappointed; "they don't fly very well, and almost always fall right down."

"Yes," said the old gentleman, "that is because the paper that buoys it up by the wind blowing against its flat surface is too thick and heavy as compared to its size. The thinner and lighter the paper the better your Parachute will fly. But the Spider constructs a much better aërial machine by climbing up to the top of some rail or tuft of grass and sending out such thin, light lines, that the ascending currents of air carry them bodily upward; as the thistle-down or seed of the dandelion is carried into the atmosphere by the action of the air upon its radiating envelope of feathery fibres."

The old gentleman told George many pleasant anecdotes of Spiders. Among others how a celebrated man who was escaping from his enemies took refuge in a cave, before which a Spider immediately began to spin its web, and when those who were in pursuit arrived at the cave and were about to search it, they saw the Spider's web stretched unbroken across the entrance, and thereupon concluded that no one had entered. He also told him of poor captives who had tamed Spiders in their gloomy prison cells, and had found occupation and amusement where else they would have died of loneliness. And also how the example of the Spider had encouraged Robert Bruce, a Scottish nobleman and one of the heirs to the throne of Scotland, when he lay a prisoner in the Tower of London. The king of England had made war upon Scotland for the purpose of conquering that country and annexing it to his own dominions. By treachery he made Robert Bruce a prisoner, and held him as a hostage for the carrying out of certain stipulations or treaties. Here Robert languished a long time, mourning over the fate of his poor, down-trodden country, which was then being ruled over by a creature of the tyrannical English king. He had made several attempts to escape and each time had been foiled, until at last he began to despair. While he was in this gloomy state, his gaze was one day attracted to a Spider that was endeavoring to cast one of its little lines or cables from one wall of the dungeon to the other. Again and again the little creature tried and failed, yet seemingly undismayed would return to the task; at last it succeeded, and ran nimbly along the bridge it had made. Robert, who had been watching its movements with great interest, sprang to his feet another man, resolved that he would take a lesson from the Spider, and strive on. Shortly after this incident he managed to escape and made his way to his native country, where he was enabled to raise an army, with which he defeated the English in a battle which occurred at a place called Bannockburn, in Scotland. The old gentleman also told George of the Tarantula, the bite of which was supposed to cause madness that could only be cured by music.

George and his friend had passed a very pleasant day, and when they returned home in the evening and had rested and refreshed themselves, the old gentleman took George into his cabinet and showed him, as he had promised to do, preserved specimens of the Spiders he had been telling him about, besides others remarkable either for their peculiar shape, such as the one shown at No. 4 in the plate, or for the form of their nest, as at No. 5, in which the lady Spider dwells at peace with her husband, which is quite as uncommon a thing among Spiders as among us. There too he saw the Zebra Spider, which we have marked No. 5, and the large bodied Spider No. 6, also the fierce looking fellow No. 7,—all curious and beautiful in their way—besides the giant, the largest of all the Spider tribe, which was once said to prey upon the humming-bird; this Spider is called the Mygale.

The old gentleman did not tax George's patience by merely giving him accounts of insects and their ways of life, however interesting they might be in themselves, but wove them into stories, of which we will give our readers a few selections just as the old gentleman wrote them out for George's benefit, commencing with some account of the Formicans.

FORMICANS.

In the midst of various other nations there have dwelt for a long time past a pigmy people, whom learned men who have studied their manners and habits call Formicans. They are divided into tribes, and have long been celebrated for their activity and industry, and for their peculiar forms of government, both civil and military. If the size of these little folks were to be the measure of their greatness, at no time could they have pretended to compete with any of the nations over whose countries they are distributed, although in many other respects they were once the superiors of those among whom they lived. Take as an example our own country, where these Formicans now live: while the Indians passed their lives dwelling in rude huts or wigwams, built here and there in great forests, and wore as clothing the skins of the wild animals they trapped, or killed with stone-headed arrows, the Formicans lived in fortified cities, wore polished armor, and had a kind of artillery, fought great battles, kept large droves of cattle, and employed numbers of slaves. Certain tribes of these tiny people have always made and kept slaves, and always will do so, for, like the Chinese and some others, the Formicans cling to old forms and customs, and cannot be made to believe in progress and modern improvement. However, they treat their slaves very kindly, and have never been known to beat or abuse them; indeed on some occasions the slaves seem to direct the affairs of the community, and they always live on terms of perfect equality with their masters and mistresses, except in the matter of labor—for these little slaves are famous hands to work, while the rest of the community, with the exception of fighting, do nothing. In a large city these slaves are the builders, scavengers, porters, nurses of the babies, and cooks, or feeders of the grown-up free community, who are mostly, like the slaves, females—for these little people seem fully to believe in the doctrine of "woman's rights," and allow the ladies and working slave-women to do all the fighting and all the work. The warrior ladies and working slave-women form the greater part of the population, the other parts being composed of a few idle gentlemen and some two or three princesses, who, although they have no voice in the government, live in great state, each surrounded by courtiers and followed by admiring crowds. In order to keep up the supply of slaves, so necessary to their existence, the tribe of Rufans make military excursions into the countries of the neighboring tribes, take them by surprise, and, by reason of their superior strength and discipline,

(25)

conquer them and carry off their children to bring up and educate as slaves. Some of the tribes of this nation raise large herds of the queerest looking little goats or sheep that you can imagine. Some of these little sheep or goats are covered with long wool, while some are naked; a great many are of a pale green color, some kinds are pink, while others are bright yellow or sober brown; some are winged, and all have trunks like so many tiny elephants, only a great deal longer in proportion to their size. The pasture-land of a herd of these small cattle is a single rose leaf, and as one field becomes exhausted the Formicans take them up bodily and carry them to another. One queer thing about these little goats, or Aphides, as they are called, is that they lay eggs like the birds, only a great many more—so many more, in fact, that if fowls laid as many, one old speckled hen might keep the markets of the United States supplied, and have plenty to spare for the rest of the world. The Formicans take a great interest in these eggs; they collect and carry them into their houses, guard them with the greatest care, and finally, when hatched, place them where the Aphide's food is most abundant. There are two little pipes coming out of the back of each of these curious little goats, from which the Formicans get the milk or honey-dew, which is carried home and equally divided among their companions. The little goats seem to love their masters very much, and give up their milk to them to the last drop. They are very merry little things, and may be often seen, as one in the picture, kicking up and sprawling about in all sorts of awkward ways, just for the fun of it. There is an ugly little black fly that troubles the Aphides very much by stinging them and laying an egg in the wound, from which egg a gnat is born which eats the poor little Aphis, leaving nothing but a hollow shell; but if any of the Formicans are with the herd, they drive away these flies.

These little Formican folks are very good to their children; they never leave them for a moment until the time comes when they must leave them forever—for the young Formicans at a certain age always go off to seek their fortunes, and found colonies and cities of their own in distant lands. But while the little ones are at home they are continually being caressed by their nurses, who lead them about, feeding and cleaning them, and when the little ones go out into the world are very reluctant to part with them. There is much more that might be told about these wonderful little creatures; but we hope enough has been said to make our little readers look around and see for themselves how wonderful are all of God's creations, and to learn that none of his works are beneath their notice.

APIANS.

Among the strange little folks who inhabit this earth, there are none more wonderful in every respect than the Apians. They are like the Formicans in their industrious habits, in the care they bestow upon their young, and in the fact that the females carry on the government and do all the work. I will tell you a story about them, which will show you what sort of creatures they are, and what strange laws and customs they have—a story which, unlike a great many of the accounts given in your histories of affairs and persons belonging to the human race, may be depended upon as strictly true.

A colony of these little Apians once established themselves in a beautiful grove surrounded by flowering fields, in the midst of which they began to build their city. They went about it in a very business-like way indeed; they divided the work up among themselves, and each one attended to her own part, and did not trouble herself to order the others around, nor fret and worry because somebody else was not doing her share. A part employed themselves in collecting building materials; but as these little folks were much too delicate to use stone or brick in the construction of their dwellings, they made their clay and plaster out of the powder-dust which they found on the inside of flowers and which they mixed with honey. Each little Apian (one of whom will be seen at Fig. 1 on our colored plate,) was furnished with a basket and brush for the purpose of collecting this powder, and very busy they made themselves, coming and going continually, and never resting until great

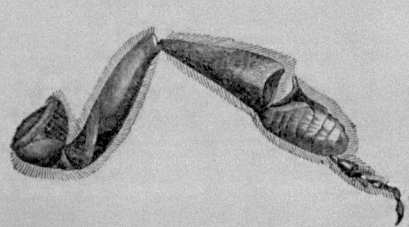

BEE'S LEG, SHOWING POLLEN BASKET

shapeless masses of the material, like the piles of brick we see in front of unfinished buildings, were ready for the masons. Soon the plans of buildings were marked out, foundations were raised, and under the busy hands of the little Apian laborers arose, as if by magic, glittering walls and towers and spacious storehouses, marvels of skillful workmanship, built in the peculiar style of architecture belonging to the race. As soon as the houses were ready, the Apians proceeded to fill them with

(27)

the dainty stores of provisions which they gathered from the honey-suckles, violets, clover-blossoms, and wild flowers. Some of the little folks, who were so busy that they really had no time to stop and take a regular lunch, were met and fed by their companions, who also went around among the masons and gave them their dinners. Others stationed themselves as sentinels at the gates of the newly-built city, and carefully examined every fresh arrival, or relieved of their burdens other Apians in a hurry to be off again. Here might be seen an Apian engaged in a hand-to-hand combat with some rash intruder; further on, the surveyors of the city clearing the passages of everything that might be in the way, or harmful to the health of the inhabitants; at another point, the workers were occupied in carrying out the dead body of one of their companions. All the outlets were crowded with Apians coming in and going out. The gates were hardly wide enough for the hurrying, busy throng; but well it was for the Apians that the gates of their city were narrow, for though they guarded them so well, and were so careful to close them at night, they were constantly besieged by thieves and robbers, who sometimes forced an entrance to feed upon the dainties the careful Apians had collected. An old giant, at least a dozen times as large as one of the poor little Apians, a terrible, old, big-bodied fellow, with a death's-head emblazoned on his back as a coat-of-arms, presented himself at one time and seemed disposed to force an entrance. In vain the sentinel angrily remonstrated, drew his flashing blade, and called his companions to the rescue; the odious monster merely squeaked out a dismal cry of defiance. The poor Apians strove with their sharp little weapons to pierce his thick hide, but without success; they retired with blunted swords and dispersed in dismay, and the huge creature actually forced his way into the city. Here, however, he was met by fresh enemies, who fearlessly threw themselves upon him, and, getting him wedged in a narrow place, kept him at bay until the masons arrived, who forthwith proceeded to build a prison around the fellow. So industrious were they, and so quickly the work went on, that the intruder soon found himself walled in and covered up—imprisoned and buried in a living tomb. While all this was going on, another foe, taking advantage of the confusion, came bearing an impenetrable house upon his back, into which he retired at the attack of the Apians. The cunning little things soon made him draw in his horns, and after chasing him into his house, sent for the strongest glue in the city and sealed up his door so that he never got out again. Having built their city and relieved themselves of their enemies, the Apians lived a busy, pleasant life for a long time.

As I have said before, these little folks had strange laws and customs, and, as is the case with fairy people generally, the women had the most to do and to say about everything. In fact there is not much that can be said in favor of the gentlemen of Apia. (See Fig. 2, colored plate.) Continually hanging about the palace where the queen resided—for the Apian law does not admit of a king—they were above soiling their hands with any honest work. Like courtiers and fine gentlemen as they were, they passed their time in eating, drinking, and waiting upon her majesty, the "mother," as her title goes in Apia. No less than four hundred of these lazy rascals lounged about the city all day, content to spend a brief season in idleness and luxury, a season that is always sure to end disastrously, for, shocking as it may appear, it is one of the laws of Apia that the gentlemen at stated times shall be put to a violent death. The queen, like a sort of female Bluebeard, when she ceases to take any further pleasure in the company of these gentlemen, excites the already indignant laborers against them to such an extent that they rush upon the poor nobles in crowds, and not being allowed to wear swords like the rest of the community, and having no means of defense, the helpless fellows are crushed and slaughtered without mercy. The Apians always obeyed their queen (who will be seen at Fig. 3 on colored plate,) in every particular when she chose to exert her authority; but she generally left the affairs of state, the enforcement of the laws, and the punishment of offenders to the people, preferring to sit in state, caressed and petted by favorite attendants, and surrounded by crowds of admirers. The Apian ladies nursed with motherly care and fondness the children of the queen, (see Fig. 4 of the plate,) who, always having a large family, kept only a few in her palace, and gave out the rest for adoption. It has always been a rule in Apia that these poor children be fed on coarse, common food, and confined in close apartments, (see Fig. 5,) so that they never arrived at their full growth. As soon as they were old enough they were sent out to work with the rest, and were in no wise different or to be distinguished from the other laborers belonging to the community. The children who were retained for future queens were treated very differently; they were lodged in large and elegant nurseries, (see Fig. 6,) slept in luxurious cots, and were fed upon a particular kind of food called "royal jelly," which was carefully made of flower juices. This precious article was of such a nourishing and exhilarating nature that it developed the little creature who fed upon it into a being quite different from an ordinary inhabitant of the city—expanding her intellect, and fitting her in every way for the exalted position she was to occupy.

One bright day, when the butterflies were restlessly fluttering from flower to flower, eagerly seeking to quench their thirst with such stray drops of dew as might have escaped being dried up by the sun, and the cicada had begun his shrill song in the tree-top, the city of Apia was in great confusion. The fixed order and strict police regulations which had so long governed the community, seemed for once to be entirely broken up and disregarded. The inhabitants of the place, whose number had increased to such an extent that the city limits could scarcely contain them, now rushed about as if distracted. The sentinels no longer kept at their posts, and the streets were filled with a multitude whose angry mutterings had now swelled to a fierce, discordant roar of popular discontent.

Some momentous event was evidently about to take place. The palace itself was left unguarded, and the queen, no longer regarded with reverence, seemed to have fallen into disgrace. Brought up in luxury and idleness, caressed and petted by all around her, her wishes anticipated, waited upon and followed by crowds of nobles and faithful attendants, loved as a mother and almost worshipped as a god, the queen now found herself totally neglected. Hoarse cries were heard, proclaiming that a faction demanded a new sovereign. Astonished, grieved, and enraged she sought to frustrate their plans by the destruction of her children. Her attendants, forgetting the sacredness of her person, threw themselves before her, vainly attempting to bar her way. Disregarding their endeavors, she rushed to the nursery that held the royal children, tore aside the curtains of their beds, and had she not been opposed by the faithful nurses in attendance, she would doutless have killed the sleeping innocents. Finding herself foiled in this attempt, she suddenly raised herself to her full height, and uttered a peculiar cry. It was a cry of strange force and meaning—none but an Apian understood it and none but an Apian felt its power. The people about her, awe-struck and submissive, fell back and bowed their heads in silence, for their queen was now, in every respect, a queen again. With a stately step she walked through the crowd assembled around the palace, and, looking back, repeated the cry which none but an Apian queen could utter; it contained a command which an Apian dared not disobey. A large party immediately separated themselves from the mob and followed the queen, but no longer offered to molest her. She led them in a constantly increasing train to the gate of the city, where they rested outside of the walls. Parties here started off at her command in search of a spot whereon to found a new colony, while those who remained behind gradually swelled in numbers by fresh desertions from the city. The insulted queen, with half the nation, left the unfortunate city to its fate—wheeling off in regular ranks and shouting in triumph, as the pioneers she had sent out returned with news of a safe and happy refuge.

Within the city walls confusion and disorder subsided. The sentinels resumed their guard, looking tired, it is true, but still standing bravely at their posts. The nurses went back to their infant charges, and tried to make up in care and tenderness for their desertion in the hour of danger, almost all of them having left their places to join in the tumult. Among the few faithful ones were the nurses who had so bravely defended their charges from the enraged queen, when that royal lady, forgetting in her mad jealousy and thirst for revenge all love for her offspring, and well knowing that the Apians could not get along without a queen, would have killed her daughters. In the streets, recently the scene of so much noise and tumult, the people gathered quietly into little knots, evidently talking over the events of the morning, and laying out plans for the future. It was well known that one of the young princesses would soon arrive at the proper age, when she would emerge from the seclusion of the royal nursery and take her place as reigning queen of the Apians, and until that time arrived they could not settle down to their accustomed work. The young princess was watched and guarded day and night, and fed continually upon the royal jelly. The time had almost arrived, and the people were on tip-toe of expectation. Everything was neglected, for nothing could be thought of but the expected event. The young queen was the only topic of conversation that had any interest for the inhabitants of the city.

At last dawned the eventful day. Crowds of citizens hurried toward the palace to witness the coronation. The ladies in waiting arrayed themselves in their best attire, and prepared to receive their young queen. The people brought rare gifts of flowery essences, sweetmeats, and sweet-smelling ointments. At the appointed time the throng, hushed in earnest expectation, directed their gaze to the spot where the young queen was to appear for the first time. A door opened; there was a flutter of silken garments, and a beautiful being stood before them, her lovely limbs clothed in light, gauzy drapery. There was a loud shout of applause from the people, and then everyone stared with amazement—for, instead of one, there were two beautiful queens standing before them. What was to be done? Two queens at one and the same time was an unheard of thing in Apia. How could such a dreadful mistake have happened? How it came to pass that this circumstance had not been known and provided against, no one ever knew. What was to be done? They were not long to remain in doubt. The nobility of Apia had always been a jealous, revengeful race, and these two young ladies were seemingly no exception to the rule. They looked at each other with disdain, tossed their pretty heads, stamped with their little feet, and then, growing more angry, advanced a step nearer to each other, drew their sharp daggers from their sheaths, and sprang together with uplifted weapons. They were equally matched, and as each saw the other's dagger about to pierce her, they shuddered and sprang apart. For an instant they seemed dismayed; but, cheered on by the people, they rushed at each other again with renewed force, with the same result as before. With a flutter of rage and shame they turned and were about to fly from the scene, when the people seized them, and forced them to fight it out then and there—which showed that the Apians were a much more sensible race than our own, who, instead of making kings and queens fight their own battles, take sides and lose fortunes and lives in quarrels with which we have personally nothing to do. The rival queens hesitated a moment, and then with one wild cry renewed the combat. There was a glitter in the air, a moan of anguish, and they both fell, pierced to the heart.

Now was there mourning indeed among the Apians. Now they were queenless and forsaken. Stupefied with grief and amazement, a mournful wail of sorrow and lamentation arose, where a few moments before all had been gladness and rejoicing. But the brave-hearted Apians soon aroused themselves from their stupor. Not long did they indulge in useless sorrow. They quickly determined what was to be done. The palace was cleared, the corpses of the unfortunate queens were borne away, and order was again restored. It was discovered that there were no more royal heiresses to the crown—for the nurses had so neglected their charges in the general excitement that almost all of them had died, and the few still living evidently would not long survive their sisters. The clear-sighted Apians, however, were at no loss to know what course to pursue. It had long been a custom among them in similar cases to select infants from among the common people, and rear them as they did their royal nurselings. Workmen immediately set about tearing down some common dwellings, and so careless were they in their haste, that several infants were crushed in the ruins. They began to build on this cleared space an elegant suite of royal nurseries, which, when finished, were furnished with everything needful for queens, and contained soft luxurious cradles and stores of royal jelly. When all this was done, several of the youngest infants that could be procured were selected and conveyed to these apartments, to be carefully nursed and fed upon the food prepared for them, until they grew out of all resemblance to their common sisters, and were fitted for the station that one of them was destined to occupy. All of this took time, of course, and the people of Apia showed very plainly their want of a ruler. The workers were not steady; frequent robberies and murders occurred in the very streets of the city; the store-houses, instead of being replenished, were frequently plundered of their rich stores; and so careless had the guard become, that an enemy, a frightful creature was not only allowed to come inside the gates, but to penetrate far into the interior of the city. A cry of alarm was raised, and every Apian drew her sword and rushed upon the monster. Fortunately, unlike the giant of the death's head, or the strong man who carried the house, this creature had neither a tough hide nor a refuge into which it could retire; but notwithstanding this, some of the poor Apians sank to the ground to rise no more before the monster was overcome. It is further said, that even some of the poor nobles of the court put their hands to their sides for swords, but, finding none, sank back in confusion and hid themselves in the palace. When the intruding robber at last sank to the earth pierced by a hundred darts, the Apians proceeded to embalm the body, and there it stood a lasting monument to their disgrace.

When at last the time came for their new-made queen to come forth among them, she appeared in every respect like their former beloved mistress. The nobles crowded around her, and paid her every attention. The maids of honor caressed her, waited upon her, and fed her with delicate food. But Apia was destined never again to occupy her proud place among the surrounding nations. The queen became listless, took no interest in her nursery, paid no attention to her admirers, and, finally, seemed to sink into a decline. No princesses were born; what few children she had were all males, more good-for-nothing, if possible, than the older ones, who, having no one to order their execution, overran the city, and imposed upon everybody. The poor work-women, having no little girls given them to rear, soon became discouraged and tired out; some died, some deserted the city and went in search of a quiet place of refuge, while others stayed at home and lived on the stores which had been put away for future use. They left off working, and soon had nothing left to live upon, and the once boasted queendom of Apia was a queendom no more, but a ruined city, noted for theft and murder. Hundreds died of famine, and no one took the trouble to bury the dead. The beautiful walls crumbled, the glittering towers fell; and the once happy city of Apia, a prey to the spirits of violence and jealousy, was a thing of the past.

APIANS. (CONTINUED.)

There are other tribes of Apians than those an account of whom has been given in the history of the rival queens, and their manners and customs are different, as the manners and customs of other nations are different from ours. Some of them build houses of wood, others of stone, and still others of mud and plaster, and some dainty little fellows use as building material the petals of the scarlet poppy. There are tribes of carpenters, upholsterers, masons, and miners, who ply their tiny trades far more skillfully and with more perfect tools than any workman of our own race. The little carpenter, for instance, (see Fig. 1 of colored plate,) who always dresses in a beautiful violet uniform

BORERS.

from head to foot, selects an upright piece of timber for her purpose, and with a couple of queer looking tools, which you can see in the picture here, and which look like a sort of patent combined awl and chisel, she bores into the wood a hole or tunnel in a slanting direction, and big enough for her to crawl into. When this is done, she turns to one side and digs away into the solid wood about twelve or fifteen times her own length, in a line that is even or parallel with the outside. This little Apian, or *Xylocopea Violacea*, as the learned men call her, has gained nothing from former experience or practice in house-building, for she builds only one house during her whole life ; but that house is as complete and finished as if she had built a hundred previously. She has no pattern or plans before her, but the Creator of all things has impressed a plan upon her mind, which she can follow without scale or compass. She has but a couple of sharp little tools to work with, and yet she hollows out a passage with greater ease than the workman who bores into the earth for water, with tools made for that particular purpose. To do as much work as one of these little creatures, a man, taking into account his immense size as compared with them, would have to dig a passage ninety feet long into solid wood. Our little Apian leaves no chips, nor does she scatter about the saw-dust, but uses up every scrap in her building. Every grain or atom of saw-dust and fibre of wood separated from the log or post in which she works out her house, is carefully gathered up and stored for future use a short distance from the spot where she is working. When at last she has completed her long gallery and smoothed and polished every part of it, she has a very nice piece of joinery to execute, which would indeed puzzle a human workman. Of the scraps of wood she

(34)

forms the floor of her house, and when this is done she proceeds, after the manner of her tribe, to place a baby in the lowest chamber, and then covers the little one up with bread and honey. One would suppose that the baby would be crushed and smothered by this sort of treatment, but it does not receive the least injury, and eats away at its store of provisions until it is exhausted, when, being old enough by that time to seek its own fortune, it opens the door and leaves the house forever. The mother, after she has placed the baby in the chamber, proceeds to build the ceiling, which she does by taking the pieces of wood she has saved and fitting them nicely together, beginning at the wall, and fastening a ring around the whole room with a sort of glue with which she is provided, and then gluing another circle on the inside of the one she has made until the whole is completed, (see No. 2,) when she places another baby upon it. When her house or nursery is full, and she has provided for all her children, whom she never expects or hopes to see again, her work is done, and she goes away to die.

A tribe of Apians, whose name is longer and harder to pronounce, the *Me-ga-chi-le Cen-tun-cu-lar-is*, have another sort of house. They are the upholsterers among the Apians, as the folks who wear violet are the carpenters. Some families of this tribe are makers of tapestry ; others carpet their dwellings and cover the walls with material cut out of rose leaves, while others shear the soft down from the stems and leaves of certain plants to form beds and make cushions. The first of these lines the cavern which serves her for a home with scarlet velvet cut from the poppy flowers. If the piece she has cut is found to be too large, she trims it to fit, much more nicely and perfectly than we could do with the sharpest scissors. When she has in this manner hung the walls of her house with the splendid scarlet tapestry, of which she is not sparing, for she extends it even beyond the entrance, she fills the house with the pollen of flowers mixed with honey, to more than her own height, and in this magazine of provisions she places her baby, and over it folds the tapestry of poppy petals from above.

The tapestry maker, however, is satisfied with beautifying the inside of her house. She does not misplace ornaments like the house builders of our race. She wishes her children's home to be secure as well as elegant, so she leaves no outside show of work to attract thieves and house-breakers. She covers her tapestried house on all sides with common earth, and leaves her children in their velvet cots, quite sure that no plunderer will find them. In the large colored picture, Nos. 3, can be seen this little tapestry maker, and at No. 4 her small house, built of rose leaves, with each little chamber full of rose-colored conserves, and with a floor cut as truly into a circle as could be done with a pair of compasses, and so formed and adjusted that each and every part seems to strengthen the whole.

One tribe of masons build their habitations of plaster, sand, clay, and small gravel, but they will not work one stroke when they can avoid it, and in many cases show a great deal of cunning in saving themselves labor. Lying hidden under hedges, bushes, and grass, are to be found the shells of different kinds of snails, such as the common garden snail and the banded snail. These shells this Apian thinks are as good as ready-made burrows, and she uses them accordingly. She goes to the further end of the shell, builds a chamber, and fills it with pollen and honey, another chamber is made and yet another, until the shell is nearly filled. As the shell widens, the *Osmia*, as she is called, (see No. 5,) places the chambers side by side, and when quite near the mouth she builds the chambers sideways to save space, and finally fills up the entrance with crumbs of dirt, pieces of sticks, and little pebbles, all fastened together with a strong, water-proof glue.

There is one kind of corpulent, burly-bodied Apian who carries a sword and wears a gold-banded uniform. (See Nos. 6.) She has, however, nothing like the amount of skill, capacity, or usefulness of her sisters who live in cities. People call her "humble," but she is, I think, altogether too vain, pompous and noisy to merit the name. Her real name is *Bombus*, and it is a good name for her, because it sounds so much like *bombast*. She has a kind of an under-ground place she calls her house, with a long, dark, and crooked passage-way leading out to daylight. Instead of the beautiful six-sided chambers the city Apian builds to hold her stores, the *Bombus* keeps her food in a lot of wide-mouthed jars, or pots, standing or lying around or loosely piled up on one another. (See No. 7.) Odd as it may appear, one can never be sure until it is opened, whether a jar contains honey or a young one, for these Apians, having nothing better for cradles, put their babies into jars, like so many of Ali Baba's forty thieves; or as I have heard the Chinese sometimes do.

VESPIANS

Besides the Apians, there is another nation, also divided up into tribes and families, called the Vespians. They are bright, nervous, fidgety little folks, with such quick tempers and such sharp swords that it is rather dangerous to have anything to do with them. They are of a slim and elegant form, and always dressed in burnished armor. Perhaps you know that a long time ago people used to write on prepared skins of animals, on slates or tablets, or slabs of metal spread over with a thin coating of wax, which those who wished to write scratched into with a sharply pointed instrument called a Stylus. Sometimes stone was used to write upon: Moses wrote the Ten Commandments upon stone. But a long time before our race had invented paper, the Vespians knew how to make it. They are the oldest paper-makers in the world. A gentleman who had carefully watched one of them working at her trade on his window-sash, gives a description of the process: With the tools furnished her by nature, she separated little bits or fibres of wood about a tenth of an inch long and as fine as a hair; these she bruised into a sort of a lint. All this the careful naturalist imitated by paring and bruising the wood from the same window-sash with his penknife, until he had succeeded in making a little bundle of fibres that could hardly be distinguished from the one made by the little Vespian. The bundle is then taken to the city in course of construction—for the Vespians like the Apians live in cities—and is well moistened with a kind of paste and spread over the yet unfinished walls, where it forms a thick streak; she then goes forward a second time, and moving slowly backward again presses the streak between the implements with which she is provided, thinning it out its whole length. This movement is repeated until the streak is of the required thickness, which object is not attained until she has gone over her work five or six times. She does not return to the same spot with her next load of fibres, but goes to another part of the building, thus giving the part first worked upon an opportunity to dry and harden before going on with that particular spot. Perhaps the wood used at the commencement was of a dark color, the next lot of fibre may have been taken from a light colored wood, and the next from a medium between the two, thus giving a pretty, variegated appearance to the work. When the dwelling place of a whole tribe is completed, it looks like the figure at the right in the colored picture, which, in order to show its interior construction, we have cut down through the middle and placed upon a tree. There are other Vespians who build more perfect and beautiful homes; but those who are here represented are very skillful workers, and will do as a sample of the others.

One of these little Amazons, a lone widow, begins the future home of the tribe. She first makes two or three little paper huts or chambers, which she gradually increases in number until she has built quite a little village. In each of these chambers she places a young Vespian, whom she daily feeds, as birds feed their nestlings. In a short time quite a number of Vespians are sufficiently grown to help their mother with her work—and hard work it must be to build so many huts and fill so many hungry mouths. However, no sooner do her good little girls find themselves strong enough, than they set to work in right good earnest to perform their share. The first thing they do is to set about building more little chambers for future infant Vespians to live in; then they nurse and feed with unwearying care their younger sisters, and are never tired of collecting the choicest and sweetest food for them. They visit the grocer's sugar casks; they rob the Apian citizens; they despoil the plum tree of its choicest produce ; and, on coming home, flit from chamber to chamber, giving each restless, craving little one its portion. The larger children need stronger food ; for these they bring home bits of meat stolen from butchers' stalls, and wild game such as captured flies and spiders.

The Vespians are always busy, for no sooner has one set of little ones grown up and joined them than another claims their care. The lone widow who was the last and first of her tribe, before the summer has gone finds herself the queen-mother of thousands.

The gentlemen of Vespia behave themselves much better than those of Apia. They are not above helping their more delicate sisters in doing the rougher work, consequently, I have no doubt they are much more respected.

As we have land animals and water animals, so we have land and water insects ; and in the chapters following our little readers will find a true account of the appearance and habits of the aquatic tribes.

ORCHIDS.

At last the chill winds of autumn, blighting the blossoms and turning the trees from green to scarlet, yellow and crimson, before stripping them altogether, announced that cold weather was at hand, and George heard with regret his father's determination to spend the winter in the great city. As he thought of the fields he was about to leave, once so green and pleasant; the brooks where he had fished and dredged with his old friend to find minnows and larvæ for the aquarium; the woods where he had gathered wild flowers and chased butterflies, the tears came into his eyes in spite of his efforts to restrain them, and he wished that it might always be summer, and that he might always live in the country. The old gentleman, to whom the wish was expressed as he received George into his study for the last time, took the little fellow upon his knee and told him of the pleasures awaiting him in the city, of the many objects of interest there, and promised him that if he could spare the time he would come and point them out to him there, and tell him about them as he had told him of those in the country. He finally brought up other subjects to make the little fellow forget the pain of parting, and said: "By the way, George, I am glad you are here to-day, for I have a puzzle-picture to show you, a very curious affair, such as I think you never saw before." We reproduce the old gentleman's picture, with which our young readers, if they choose, may puzzle their friends. It was quite large, and being brightly colored, George thought it very pretty.

"Now, George," said the old gentleman, smiling, "you may have heard of the man who had a panorama so badly painted that he had to say to his audience, 'Ladies and gentlemen! this is a picture of Dan'l in the Lion's Den; you can tell Dan'l from the Lions by the green cotton umberill he carries under his left arm.' The difficulty in this picture is that there is not even 'a green cotton umberill' as a distinguishing mark; and further, that the truer the picture is to nature the greater is the difficulty, which is, in this case, to tell the flowers from the insects."

In trying to do this George made a great many amusing mistakes, which were all corrected, and he began to see his way clear as his father entered the study. Here was a new source of diversion, and George attacked him at once, while the old gentleman sat by, almost as much amused as the boy.

"Point out the flowers and the insects?" said George's father, not suspecting there was a trap; "well, I should think that was no such a hard matter."

"What a queer looking butterfly that is;" and he put his finger straight on No. 4.

"I knew he'd do it!" cried George, almost screaming with delight, and clapping his hands. "I did it, too. That ain't no butterfly!"

"'Ain't no butterfly,' George?" said the old gentleman.

"Ain't any butterfly, then," said George, a little sobered.

"And if it ain't a butterfly, what is it, pray?" asked his father.

"It's an Orchard!" cried George: "Its an Orchard!"

"What is it?" asked his father, hastily.

"An Orchid, he means," said the old gentleman, smiling; "a flower of the Orchis, or air-plant family. Many of these flowers have a tendency to imitate various objects in nature; some, as you see, are like butterflies, others like spiders, as at No. 4; still others, within a cup of the purest white, the perfect form of a dove. As the flowers imitate insects, so the insects appear to imitate flowers, as in the case of the *Kal-li-ma Pa-ra-lec-ta*," and he placed his finger upon No. 1. "You see how much it looks like a leaf?"

"It does indeed;" said George's father, putting on his eye-glasses to look at it more closely. "Bless me! I thought it was one."

"The folded in, or upper part of the wings," said the old gentleman, "are of a rich purple color, with orange and ash-colored markings, making a very showy appearance when flying about, but when it alights it is very difficult to find. It rests with its wings shut closely together, with all other parts but its legs and the under part of its wings concealed; thus appearing of an ash or ashy-brown color, it very closely resembles a dried leaf, and the position it takes upon a stem or branch serves to increase the illusion, the shape of the wings with tails being like a leaf-stalk, and the markings resembling the mid-rib and veining of the leaf."

"What would you suppose these to be?" said the old gentleman, his finger passing to No. 9.

"Why," replied his visitor, with extreme caution, afraid of being again taken a-back, "they look like—like—not Orchids, certainly, nor butterflies. You cannot mean these twigs?"

"Yes, but I do;" said the Professor, triumphantly. "Those are *Di-a-phom-e-ra Fem-o-ra-ta*."

"Ah! indeed!" said George's father, catching his breath.

"Yes," said the old gentleman; "that is what the scientific people call it. The long, cylindrical, wingless body of this insect is supported by slender legs, and really looks so much like a twig as to have been casually picked up to make a tooth-pick from."

"Ugh!" said George and his father, involuntarily.

"They are green when young," continued the old gentleman, "and afterwards become brown, like an old twig. Sometimes these sticks are replaced by leaves, as in the case of the East Indian Leaf Insect, the *Phyllium*," and he directed their attention to No. 2.

"Ah!" said George's father, "I rather suspected our friend, Phil—what—ah! yes, Phyllium; but I did not like to mention him for fear he might turn out to be an Orchid, or something of the sort."

"There are several of these insects, of which the colored picture contains two—a larger and a smaller one, Nos. 2 and 6," said the old gentleman.

"I will venture to ask what these queer little worm-shaped creatures are, at No. 7," said George's father.

"Those are not worms at all; they are of vegetable origin," was the answer.

"What! wrong again?" said his visitor.

"Yes," replied the old gentleman. "That is the Snake Nut, from Demerara. The artist has taken the liberty of introducing a couple of eyes, that may represent accidental depressions in the kernel."

"I suppose it has a great, long name," said George, "ending in *us* or *um*?"

"Yes," said the old gentleman, "it has a very long name indeed: *Ophir-is-car-you Par-a-dux-um*."

"Well," remarked George, thoughtfully regarding the picture, "Something Pair-of-ducks-um, I shall know you again."

"Here is another twig that crawls, eats, and possesses animal life," said our old friend, pointing out No. 8. "He is a looper, and turns into the Swallowtail Moth; you will see him again at No. 12."

"Oh! I know the fellow," said George's father; "he has a trick of letting himself down from the Maple trees and swinging in our faces as we may be passing. I know him for an uninvited and unwelcome guest who is entirely too familiar for comfort."

"Here," remarked the old gentleman, pointing out No. 10, "is an insect that seems likely to escape notice.

"Yes, sir," said George, "and you have'nt told us anything about No. 4 and No. 5."

"Oh, those," replied his friend, "are two specimens of the Butterfly flower, of which I have already spoken; but the little fellow at No. 10 is perhaps the most interesting member of his family, and, unlike the others, is remarkable not only on account of his odd appearance, but for his queer habits and actions. His name is *Mantis*, and he is called the praying Mantis, because he seems to fold what answers him in the place of hands, and assumes an attitude of the deepest devotion. Let any poor, unsuspecting insect, however, deceived by his apparent inoffensiveness, venture near, and he shows himself the ferocious monster and hypocrite he really is, by seizing his victim and remorse-lessly devouring it upon the spot. These insects are extremely savage, and when placed together will fight with the greatest fury, until the weaker or less skillful falls a prey to his antagonist, who immediately dines off of his unfortunate brother. In their combats these creatures strike and parry with the edge of their fore claws, as if they were fighting a duel with swords; indeed the natives of China and Japan, I am told, set them fighting, as some people, even in our own enlightened country, do dogs and cocks, to stake money on the result."

In conclusion, the old gentleman spoke very eloquently and beautifully of the part of God's creation that had occupied so much of his little friend's attention during the summer. "Nature," said he, "in her smaller works exhibits a delicacy of finish, a brilliancy of texture and color, a com-plexity and variety of structure, far surpassing even her grander and more enduring creations. Certainly the wildest, most grotesque and strangely beautiful of her productions are to be found in the insect world, which, to those who interest themselves in it, is a land of faries, replete with strange and sudden transformations, apparent miracles, and weird beings, far more surprising than the efforts of the human imagination in romance, or tales of magician and genii have ever been able to produce. Its wonders are inexhaustible, and as yet but very imperfectly explored, and, at present at least, of all branches of natural science it is, perhaps, the least systematically cultivated. If any one wishes to hand down his name to posterity as a great discoverer in unknown realms of creation, I do not know a field that is so likely to reward his exertions with rich and surprising results as the great, un-explored tracts of the insect world."

If our little readers care for a further acquaintance with George and his old friend, they can meet them again in the other books of this series, where a further account is given of the wonders of creation, and the strange and beautiful facts, which, in books of science, are hidden under such loads of hard names and dry reading.

FANTASY.

THE ADVENTURES

OF

LITTLE FANTASY

AMONG THE

WATER DEVILS.

LIST OF ILLUSTRATIONS.

FANTASY.

ONCE upon a time there lived, deep in the green heart of the forest, a little elfin creature whose name was Fantasy. This little fellow lived in the hollow of a beautiful straight oak tree, where some little squirrel had intended to lay by its store for the winter; but Fantasy had driven out the squirrel and taken possession of the place himself. In fact no squirrel could have had the heart to scold the little fellow, he was such a mite of a thing, with bright, sparkling eyes, and a sweet smile on his cunning face; and when he laughed right out, which was not seldom, his pointed white teeth showed so prettily that one had to laugh for sympathy. He was a lazy little fellow, too; he would not work, but danced and played all day long. He would gather honey from the flowers like any bee, only he never laid by any for i.   use; and he quenched his thirst at the first dew-drop he met. After feasting on such choice b s as this, he would go home to his hollow in the oak and sleep until the moonlight shone down through the green leaves, and then he was ready for fun. Jumping up from his bed of butterfly-down, sometimes he would steal up to some pretty little bird asleep in its nest, and catching its beak would give it such a pull that poor birdie would fall to the ground almost frightened to death. Then he would take the petal of a flower, twisted into the shape

of a goblet, and filling it to the brim with dew, would empty it down upon the unsuspecting head of some small creature of the forest, who thought himself secure in the shelter of a friendly leaf. All such tricks, and many more than I can tell, would our little elf perform, much to the grief of a wise old fairy, named Science, who tried to bring him up in the way he should go. She it was who lined his little house with soft green moss, made him a bed of down from the breast of the humming-bird, covered with the silken wool of moths and butterflies, spread it with rose-leaf blankets, and dressed him in a hunting suit of green and gold, and a helmet made from the shell of a bright, golden-backed beetle, with a vizor that he could draw down over his face, to shield him from the darts of any ill-disposed creature he might meet with in his woodland rambles.

Now one would think that Fantasy would have been a contented little elf, after having so much done for him; but no, he could not be satisfied; and one day horrified his fairy godmother by informing her that he was going out into the world to seek his fortune. The poor fairy, in despair, wept bitterly, and implored him to stay with her; but it was of no use, Fantasy was determined to go. Poor old Science! she had no chick nor child of her own, and had been such a blue-stocking, she never had time to think of getting married or making friends. Her only companion, beside a stupid colony of tame owls and bats that she had reared by hand, was Fantasy, and despite the naughty tricks he played her, she loved him dearly. However, as she more than half expected to see him back again in a short time, she consoled herself with the hope that he would soon get into such a medley of difficulties he would be glad to return and ask her aid. She was the more certain of this, as he had so often led her off into swamps and quicksands in order to show her some great discovery he thought he had made, and which, upon being reached, often proved nothing worth looking at; when in the end the reckless little fellow, tired out and disappointed, was glad to lay his weary head on her cold bosom, and be borne, sleeping, in her strong arms, back to his home. Nevertheless, as he was such a reckless, wandering, bright-eyed little person, he did not always deceive himself, and sometimes made discoveries that were very useful to Science, so she was generally persuaded to look at what he found to see whether it amounted to anything or not. However, he was determined now to leave her, at least for a time, and so she gave him what she thought would be of most service to him—a great deal of good advice, and, what Fantasy liked better, a magic cloak, woven by a water witch, which would save him from drowning, and a sharp little blade to defend himself from the strong, fierce, creatures, of which she said the world was full, and bidding him take good care of himself, she let him go.

Fantasy started off with a brave heart, feeling that with his little sword he could conquer everything that came in his way. He wandered along some time without seeing much to attract his attention, until he came suddenly upon a beautiful stream of water. Now Fantasy remembered that his fairy godmother had said, "Beware, Fantasy, of the water-devils;" so he looked carefully about him, up and down the broad expanse of water into which the stream spread out at his feet, peeped under the bushes, and examined every nook and corner to try to find one of these water devils, determined to kill him with his sharp little sword. He found nothing, however, and saying to himself that "the old fairy didn't know everything," he sat down on the bank of the stream to rest. While he sat there dreamily watching the tall water-flags sway slowly to the current, with the ripples playing around them in the sunlight like little serpents of silver fire, while he sat there trying to catch and understand the murmurs and whispers of the water and the leaves conversing in an under-tone together, while behind him the great woods seemed to hold their breath and listen too, as if some one had all at once said "hush!" he saw a party of the strangest little figures imaginable, come down the stream. They had queer, slender little bodies, and seemed to be dancing right on the surface of the water. Fantasy, in all his life before, had never seen such dancing. They spun round and round so fast it made one dizzy to look at them, and the strangest thing of all was that they appeared to be dancing on their heads. "Well now!" said Fantasy, drawing in his breath with pleasure and astonishment, "that is something like! I wish I could dance like that. Halloo!" he shouted; "you lively chaps there, what are your names?"

"Whirl-agigs; Whirl-agigs;" they screamed as they spun by.

"Wait a minute," cried Fantasy; "teach me to dance on my head." But they paid no attention to what he said, and went sailing down the stream.

"Well," said Fantasy disgusted, "that is polite I must say; I suspect those fellows have been drinking too much; they acted like it. But I do wish I had a boat to cross this water."

"Who is it wants a boat?" said a voice close to his side. Fantasy started and looked about him, under the bushes and up at the sky, and seeing nothing, his eyes fell on the water, and there, sure enough, he beheld the owner of the voice—a queer little fellow, dressed all in black, and shining like polished jet from top to toe.

"Pray, sir, who are you?" said Fantasy.

"I am the boatman," replied the figure; "do you want to go across?"

"Why, yes" said Fantasy "I should like to; but where is your boat?"

The little man laughed a harsh, unpleasant laugh, and said. "Oh, I will find one easy enough;" and throwing himself upon his back in the water, told Fantasy to "jump aboard;" but Fantasy stared '

"You can sit on my breast," said the black man, "and I will paddle you across."

The little elf, reckless as he was, scarcely liked to trust himself upon such a strange craft, but seeing no other way of pursuing his journey, he hesitated but a moment, before he stepped lightly upon the polished black deck of his living ship. As they started out swiftly from the shore, Fantasy discovered that his ferryman had oar-shaped feet and that his sharp head cut through the water like the prow of a boat. The little elf enjoyed his ride very much, and so far forgot his fear of his strange boatman, that he would strike him from time to time with his little hand, to make him go. Seeing that the ferryman seemed to take these liberties in good part, Fantasy felt further emboldened to ask him his name and history?

"I am called *Aquarius*," said the black, "of the nation of *Coleoptera*. I was born upon the boundaries of Algae. I can walk the earth like such creatures as you. I can swim as you see upon the water like a duck, or under the water like a fish, and I can fly in the air like a bird. I am strong, brave and handsome, a meat-eater and a creature of three elements. I wear an impenetrable armor, and I am not afraid of the great water witch herself."

"And you are a conceited fellow," thought Fantasy, but he did not say so aloud, as he did not care to offend the black, at least until he was safe ashore; besides which, his conscience told him "that people who live in glass houses should not throw stones." As they were passing near a clump of bushes, Fantasy discovered two or three boats that seemed to be sheltered under the leaves of a water plant.

"See" said he to his boatman, "those boats seem to be quite elegantly shaped; besides they are sheltered from the sun which is getting too hot for me. I would like to ride in one of them."

"Indeed you can't ride in one of those boats," said the black; "those are Madame Gnat's boats, and she uses them for nurseries. Her young children are under the decks."

"Well," retorted Fantasy, "I am pretty light weight. I am sure they can carry me as well as the children, and at any rate I am determined to try."

The boatman laughed, but said no more; and as they were now very near one of the boats, Fantasy jumped lightly into it. For a moment it rocked and tumbled so that the naughty little elf was afraid he should fall out, and he drew his water-proof cloak more closely around him. The boat however, soon became still again, too still in fact for our elf, for it ceased to move altogether. In vain Fantasy pounded and shouted, it would not move an inch, until at last, getting into a foolish little passion, he drew his sword and struck such a blow that he cut off a corner of the boat. Almost before he had time to think he had fallen from the half overturned vessel, and was sinking slowly down into the cool green water. Fantasy as he fell caught his cloak about him, and found to his surprise and delight, that it craried down with it air enough for him to breathe, so that he saw he was in no danger of drowning. He could also see around him very well, and suceeding so bravely in his adventures, he determined to walk about at his leisure under the water and amuse himself awhile, playing with the bright colored pebbles and little shells he found there.

What a beautiful world it was under the water! The sunlight, softened and subdued, came through the cool green depth and lit up the velvety, bright colored mosses that lay scattered about, or hung down from the rocks and submerged roots of the great trees, and waved gently to and fro, half showing, half hiding, deep shadowy recesses, where silvery little fish were lurking. Fantasy amused himself for some time watching the bubbles ascend as he stirred the pebbles beneath his feet, and chasing the shadows of moving objects above, as they passed, slowly or swiftly, over the bottom of the stream, across his way. Being akin to the swift creatures of the air and water, he could make his way through the denser element with much more ease and quickness than one of our own race, burdened with his large clumsy body, could hope to do. After playing about until he was tired, Fantasy came across a little cave in the rocks where the green moss looked so soft and inviting he thought he would creep down into it and rest awhile. Just as he was about to enter the cave, however, he started back in horror—for, peering at him from a corner of the cavern, he saw a hideous face, with flashing eyes, so terrible that poor Fantasy felt chilled to the heart with dread. He expected a monster to leap out to atack him; but the deformed countenance kept its stony eyes fixed upon him, and did not move. Fantasy, whose courage could not long remain quelled, soon plucked up heart at this, and asked the creature to introduce itself to him by name, at the same time feeling a great mind to cover up his ears, dreading to hear the voice that must belong to so frightful a being.

He was much surprised, on the contrary, to hear a soft, smooth tone and honied words, answer him and say, " I am quite a harmless creature; do not be frightened. Nature has given me an ugly face, but I have a good heart. I and my brothers and sisters are placed down here, in this dreary, watery world, for a short time during our innocent child-hood; but if we are good, and do our duty to the other creatures we meet with, we are sent into the world above, where we are given forms so beautiful and bright that it would dazzle your eyes to look upon us; and so strong are we then that we are named the dragons."

All the time the creature had been saying this, it had been drawing gradually nearer and nearer to Fantasy, who, by no means liking its manner or looks, had retreated backwards and kept his hand on his sword.

" Why are you afraid, you beautiful being?" said the stranger.—" I love all things that have life under the water, especially tender creatures, such as you appear to be, without shells or prickles. How lovely and fat you are. I would not harm you for the whole world. Perhaps you do not believe what I have told you. How sad is the want of mutual confidence between inhabitants of the same ditch. Ah! the time for my change is very near, when this vile shape will be cast aside, and you may be able to see for yourself. Then, indeed, instead of this ugly face and short brown body, I shall have elegant features, with eyes so bright, the sun will appear dim in comparison, and my straight, slender form, will be clothed in living garments of glittering green and gold."

Fantasy had become so interested in the description the creature gave him of what he was soon going to be, that he had allowed the horrible face to creep close to him, and while he was looking at it, he was startled and alarmed to see the front of the face fall down like a mask! Then it changed, opened, and became a sharp toothed trap, and, springing forward, the masked assassin tried to catch our little elf in his horrible machine. But Fantasy was too quick for him; with a scream of

terror he jumped aside just in time, and the deadly trap only grazed and wounded his arm and tore a large rent in his magic cloak. Poor Fantasy felt the pain, and the water rushing through the torn garment, and crying bitterly for his fairy godmother, he arose to the top of the water as soon as he could, expecting every moment to feel the trap closing over his limbs. He reached the surface of the stream in safety, however, and fortunately, as he then thought, came up just by the side of the black boatman.

"Oh do take me up, good boatman," cried the little elf; "I am almost killed." the boatman chuckled to himself, and Fantasy saw that his eyes had the same ugly look as those of the murderer under the water. He trembled with fear, but the boatman's expression changed as he told Fantasy to get aboard and he would take him ashore. Wet, shivering, and miserable enough, Fantasy crawled upon the body of the ferryman and binding up his wound lay down in the sun to dry himself. He soon became warm and comfortable; his wound ceased to pain him, and he began to be interested again in what he saw around him.

"What is that white dome that glistens like silver in the sun?" he said to the boatman.

"That," replied the ferry-man, "is the bower of the beautiful Lady Spinner. The dome that rises half way out of the water is made of the fairest and closest gossamer, spun and woven by the lady herself, who reclines beneath it at her leisure; for by a process known only to herself and family she fills her bower with air, but prevents the water from getting into it. It is very beautiful inside, all hung with silken curtains, and rocks softly in the waves."

"Oh," said Fantasy, charmed with this description, "I should so much like to visit her and see the inside of her bower, but I cannot get in at the top of the dome; besides, my magic cloak is torn so, I should become all wet in going through the water and I fear that the lady would scarcely receive me in such a plight."

"Yes she would," said the boatman; "I would tell her you are a friend of mine, and she will be glad to see you; don't doubt that you'll be welcome."

They were soon by the side of the lady's bower. Fantasy could now see what a beautiful curve its roof formed, and how fine were the silken threads of which it was woven.

"Lady Spinner!" cried the boatman, "I have brought a young gentleman to see you; he has been wounded; will you not take him into your beautiful bower?"

"The young stranger is welcome," said a voice, that Fantasy could not help thinking was anything but musical; but then, perhaps, the poor thing had a bad cold. "I will myself, help him into my bower. Put down your hands, fair sir, and I will lead you in and nurse you tenderly." Fantasy leaned down and put his hands under the water; they were seized with a strong grip, and his boatman giving him a push, he fell into the water. But oh horror! Instead of a beautiful lady in the silken bower, a horrible old witch, with leaden eyes, and long skinny arms covered with hair, held him in a close embrace and tried to draw him into her den, where Fantasy, looking, beheld the remains of murdered victims yet clinging to the silken walls. He struggled desperately, and being enveloped in the remains of his magic cloak, tore himself loose, leaving his garment in her claws. This, fortunately gave him a chance to use the weapon given him by Science, and he struck the syren with his sword. She screamed with anger, and hit, and tore him with her long claws until poor Fantasy was almost exhausted; but making a last desperate effort for his life, his right arm yet being free, he stabbed her so deeply that his sword hilt, where the one word "Wisdom" was engraved, met her body. With a groan her long, sinewy arms unclasped, and her hideous body sank out of sight.

Fantasy was terribly wounded, but he kept up bravely, and determined that he would no longer trust his deceitful boatman, so he swam slowly to the shore which was not far away. His cloak was torn in pieces and lost, he was wet through, but he rested one arm on a twig that floated by and with the other he paddled himself along. When at last he dragged himself out of the water, he had barely strength to climb the slippery bank and hide in the long grass. He wept very bitterly; wishing that he had been guided by the wise counsels of Science, and remained in his mossy nest. Tired as he was, he was still more hungry; he had not eaten anything for a long time, so, as soon as he regained sufficient strength to walk he went in search of food, trembling with fear and hiding himself at every strange noise. He had not gone far before he was fortunate enough to find some sweet honeysuckles blooming within reach ; he eagerly drank the refreshing nectar from their graceful vases, bathed his poor wounded little limbs in the dew that glistened on the grass, and having looked carefully around to see if an enemy were near, nestled down under the shadow of the honeysuckles and was

soon fast asleep. He slept a long time when, awakened by a loud rushing sound very near him he started, rubbed his eyes, and then remembering where he was, sprang to his feet in terror ; and well might he be frightened, for right before him stood a tall figure, three times his own size, with threatening mein and fierce, angry eyes, that seemed to pierce Fantasy through, they were so bright and dazzling. The stranger was dressed in glittering armor, and bore four great wings that stood out from his back like the arms of a windmill.

"Well my fine fellow," he said in a voice that sounded strangely familiar to Fantasy, "you escaped me once under the water, but you are now at my mercy and you shall die."

The little elf felt that his last moment had indeed come, for he knew the voice was that of the masked assassin—knew that the dreaded Dragon stood before him. He fell on his knees and begged for mercy.

"Mercy?" said the stranger scornfully; "who ever heard of a Dragon showing mercy? I know no mercy; nor fear except in one single instance. There is a creature not half my size, who carries a sword that is charmed—once struck by that I am overpowered; but, as I am swifter of flight than he, I am safe from the Scorpion; other creatures fear I none. I can conquer all things save truth, and from him I can escape. See those white-robed beings sporting on the water's edge; silly moths, only fit for flower gardens; they are my prey. I will fly in their direction, and the rush of my pinions will terrify the creatures half to death." Saying which, the terrible Dragon rose in the air, and, sure enough, the poor little nymphs scattered in every direction. But while the proud Dragon was laughing at the fear he inspired, he did not perceive the approach of his enemy,

the dreaded Scorpion. To late he saw his danger and attempted to escape; he was seized from behind and a deadly struggle ensued.

As soon as Fantasy saw this he sprang forward, and ran as fast as his little feet could carry him and having luckily landed on the same side of the stream he started from, he made the best of his way toward the wood that contained his nest, and never looked around or stopped to rest until, footsore, torn, bleeding and worn out, he at last reached his home in the oak tree, where he found his fairy godmother waiting for him. Poor Fantasy fell at her feet all covered with wounds, his beautiful clothes torn in pieces, and in every respect very much unlike the forward little Fantasy who had started out so bravely in the early morning to conquer the world. The good fairy nursed him and took such good care of him—being the best physician in the world—that he soon got well, and was a good, quiet little elf ever after his adventures with the terrible Water Devils.

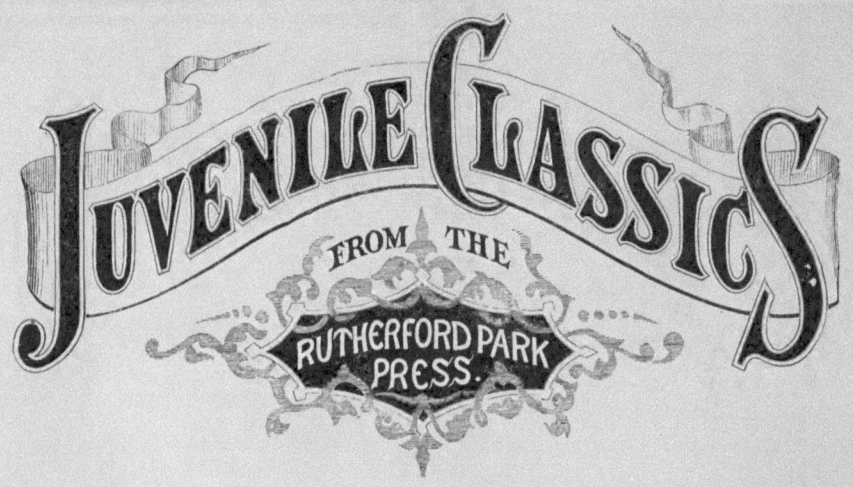

BOOKS NOW READY.

FABLES: Quarto size; compiled from Æsop, LaFontaine, and the Russian of the celebrated Kriloff. Some of these are old and favored acquaintances, while others are here published for the first time in this country. Embellished with handsome full-page illustrations, printed in colors, from characteristic designs by Stephens and others. Illuminated cover. Issued in 8 numbers, each number complete in itself. Nos. 1 and 2 now ready. Price per No. 50 cents.

TRANSFORMATION BOOKS. Three books full of funny pictures, which will afford entertainment and amusement to the children. Two sizes; large size 10 cents, small size 5 cents.

NURSERY RHYMES: with numerous colored illustration from designs by Stephens. Price 25 cents.

LITTLE WORKERS: A history of some of God's little creatures that labor without hands. By J. C. Beard. Magnificently illustrated with numerous full-page pictures, printed in oil colors, from designs by Beard. Quarto size; illuminated cover. Price $1,00.

The publishers have spared no exertions or expense in the endeavor to make this the most attractive and interesting book ever printed in this country. It is written in a style that will meet the comprehension and enchain the attention of any reader, old or young. It imparts solid and useful information in a pleasing and informal manner, especially entertaining to the child. It is a truthful and fascinating account of some of the most exquisite of our Heavenly Father's creations; teaching us his greatness even in little things. The utmost care has been taken with the pictorial matter, to the end that, not only are the objects illustrated strictly true to nature, but that each of the numerous illustrations shall be to our little readers "a thing of beauty and a joy forever."

LITTLE FANTASY: The Adventures of Little Fantasy with the Water Devils. Price 25 Cents.

SILHOUETTE SERIES: MOTHER GOOSE, AND OTHER RHYMES, PRICE 10 CENTS.

Death of Cock Robin,   House that Jack Built,
Simple Simon,   John Gilpin.